LEGEND
(in their own lunchbox)

Kim's Super Science Day

Sherryl Clark & Heath McKenzie

capstone
classroom

capstone
classroom

Legends (in Their Own Lunchbox) is published by Capstone Classroom
1710 Roe Crest Drive
North Mankato, MN 56003
www.capstoneclassroom.com

Library of Congress Cataloging-In-Publication data is available on the Library of
Congress website.

ISBN: 978-1-4966-0250-3

This edition of *Kim's Super Science Day* is published by arrangement with Macmillan
Publishers Australia Pty Ltd 2013.

Photo credits: iStockphoto.com/marlanu, **52**

This book has been officially leveled by using the F&P Text Level Gradient™
Leveling System.

Printed in China

CONTENTS

MEET the Characters

I'm Kim.
I'm an ace
reporter who
always gets
her scoop!

I'm Ella,
Kim's best friend.
I help her track
down clues.

I'm Kim's dad.
I run the local
newspaper.

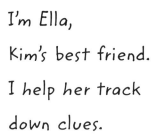

I'm Tom.
My science
project is
going to be
the best ever!

SCIENCE PROJECT
COMPETITION

Best Experiment!

FIRST PRIZE:
Family Dinner
at Smith's Café

Chapter 1

Boring Science!

Kim wasn't interested in entering the science competition, until she heard the latest news.

"Quiet!" Mrs. Brown held up her hand and Kim's class fell silent. "There is a *new* first prize. A video camera."

Kim sat up when Mrs. Brown said,
"It's been donated by Mr. Smith.
So the family dinner is now second
prize."

Kim wanted that video camera. It would make her blog amazing. It could be a video blog — a vlog!

But first she'd have to enter the competition. Everyone had been talking about their projects for weeks. Fake volcanoes. How fast can carrots grow with special fertilizer? Do plants scream when you squeeze or cut them? Super boring. She hadn't even reported on her blog about it.

Kim barely heard Mrs. Brown say that Mr. Smith would judge the competition himself this year. Kim was busy trying to dream up an amazing science project. Her brain spun like a whirligig.

At recess, she asked Ella, "What is your science project about?"

"I'm not sure yet," Ella said. "I could make a — "

Tom butted in. "I'm not telling you what I'm making," he said. "Mine is a really big secret." He grinned and mimed zipping his lips together. Then he laughed a strange laugh.

Kim shuddered. Sometimes Tom had very weird ideas about things. Like the time he'd drawn smiley faces on all the eggs in the supermarket. Or the time he'd superglued the library door shut because he wanted one of the new books first.

Grown-ups didn't like it when you did things like that.

Ella and Tom were no help. Kim was on her own.

Chapter 2
Crazy Volcanoes

That night Kim spent hours on the Internet, looking for ideas. Bubbling volcanoes. Lots of experiments on plants. More experiments on food. Who cared what size microwave made the best popcorn?

At last she found something. Invisible ink. There were several ways to make it. She tried all of them.

One way was with vinegar. Mom only had purple vinegar and it wasn't invisible at all. Dad came in and sniffed. "Mmm, salad."

THIS IS A REALLY STUPID IDEA!

"No, Dad. Invisible ink."

He looked at the page she'd written on. "I can read that. It says *This is a really stupid idea.*"

Kim was getting grumpy. Next she tried the lemon juice. That was better. At least she couldn't read it on the page.

But when she heated the paper up over a candle, the page caught on fire. She had to throw it into the sink and turn the faucet on. The smoke alarm went off.

Dad came running. "Should I call the fire department?" he asked.

"No, Dad." Kim sighed. "I was trying to heat up my invisible ink."

"Next time use a lightbulb," he suggested.

Next, Kim made invisible ink with corn starch and water. When it was dry, she took it into the living room and used Mom's reading lamp. Sure enough, the writing turned pale brown.

It was stupid. But she couldn't think of anything else.

This is my stupid science experiment using invisible ink.

When Kim went to bed, she dreamed of science experiments everywhere. Everyone was making fake volcanoes. They exploded around her in red, blue, green, and purple. She was covered in foam.

Kim woke up in a sweat. She absolutely had to think of something else. Something different — and good enough to win that camera!

Chapter 3
Tom Acts Strangely

The next day at school, Mrs. Brown held up the prize. The video camera was so shiny.

"I bet that cost more than dinner at Smith's Café," Tom said.

"I heard Mr. Smith won it in a raffle,"

Ella said. "He already has one so that's why it's a new first prize."

Kim gazed at the camera. She could just see herself filming interviews and exciting events around Blarton.

Her blog would become a famous vlog.
She'd become famous. She might film
something for *Funniest Home Movies*
and win lots of money. She could ...

"Kim!" Mrs. Brown loomed over her. "Have you done your math homework?"

"Er ... no." Kim's face was bright red. Mrs. Brown was so mean!

At recess, Ella said, "Did you decide on your science project?"

Kim nodded. "It's pretty amazing."

It wasn't. She still had no ideas. "What are you doing?"

"It's a volcano." Ella frowned. "But maybe that's too boring."

"I'm going to make something really fantastic," Kim said. But she couldn't think of anything. Maybe she would have to make a volcano, too.

When Kim got home she looked up information on volcanoes. Maybe if she made an extra large volcano, that might work. But it all looked very boring. Then she saw a link to a fountain. She clicked and saw a picture of a glowing fountain. Now that was cool! And cheap.

All she needed was a bottle of tonic water and some mints.

She asked Mom for some money and ran to the supermarket.

In one aisle, she saw Tom. He was looking at matches and firelighters, and he was giggling. That wasn't a good sign. Was he planning to burn down the school? That would be a science project nobody would ever forget! She had to know what he was up to. She sneaked up behind him and put a hand on his shoulder. "Tom."

He nearly jumped out of his sneakers. "What do you want?"

"Don't do it," Kim said. "It's not worth it."

His face turned almost purple. "You're a sneak and a tattletale."

"I'm not. I just don't want you to get into trouble."

"It's a science project!" he yelled. "Don't you dare say a word!" He ran off.

Now Kim was really worried. Should she tell somebody? But he hadn't done anything. He hadn't even bought anything in the end.

She bought her tonic water and mints and walked home, thinking.

Finally she decided not to say anything. There was no evidence. But she knew that, on the day of the science displays, she would keep a very close eye on Tom.

Chapter 4
A Sticky Situation

When Kim read the instructions again, she realized she needed a black light that made things glow.

She asked Dad. "They're expensive," he said. "How about you see how the experiment goes first?"

"Okay." She put the bottle of tonic water on the table. Would this really work? She put the whole roll of mints into the bottle, screwed on the lid and waited.

"Take the lid off," Dad said. "You can't have a fountain like that."

Kim slowly unscrewed the lid and waited. Nothing. The mints sat in the bottom, bubbling a little bit. Nothing.

Kim grabbed the bottle and shook it. Suddenly it exploded, just as Mom came in. A huge fountain of tonic water spouted out. Mom screamed. Dad yelled, "Put the lid on! Hurry!"

But it was too late.

Eventually the fountain stopped.

Mom took a step forward and her foot stuck to the floor. She looked at Kim. "The whole kitchen is sticky."

Kim was in trouble.

Two hours and six buckets of soapy water later, Mom was happy again. Kim decided the fountain was off her list.

Now what?

Dad felt sorry for her and took them all to Smith's Café for dinner. Mr. Smith made very good pizzas. Kim had a pizza with all the toppings.

Mr. Smith walked past their table. "Are you going to report on the winner of the science project competition?" he asked Dad.

"Sure," Dad said.

Mr. Smith added, "You won't forget to mention I'm donating the prizes?" He pointed. There was the camera, all shiny and new. It even had a nice black case.

"Of course," Dad said. "I can see why all the kids want to win. Even if some of them are getting *sticky* about it. Ha ha."

Kim scowled at Dad. She tried not to look at the beautiful camera, but she couldn't help it. It was like the camera was calling to her.

She had to win the prize! She would go home and keep looking for something amazing. Mom and Dad were talking about when they were young and Kim heard Mom's last words. "Lava lamps."

"What's a lava lamp?" Kim asked.

"Look it up," Dad said.

Kim groaned. He always said that. When she got home, she did a search for lava lamps. They were filled with oil and made colored shapes. There were even some videos of them. They looked really cool, like rolling lava.

Then she found a link to how to
make your own lava lamp.

INSTRUCTIONS

- Use a 2-liter bottle. Fill one quarter with water, three quarters with cooking oil.
- Let the water settle at the bottom.
- Put in 6 drops of food coloring.
- It will float down and mix with the water.
- Then add 2–3 fizzy antacid tablets and watch the oil bubble and roll!

(Put a flashlight underneath to light it up like a lamp.)

Yes! That was it! The perfect science
project. She would definitely win
with this!

Chapter 5
Eruptions Everywhere!

By the time the science display day arrived, Kim had made three lava lamps. She took her third and best one in a box to the competition hall.

Everyone else had their projects in boxes too, even Tom.

Kim watched Tom closely but he just put his box on the table and stood next to it.

Mr. Smith arrived, dressed in his best safari suit. Mrs. Brown said, "Everyone put your projects out on the table for the judging, please."

Soon the tables were full of all kinds of experiments. Kim counted four volcanoes, six trays of plants, and a huge mountain of popcorn. Ella had made a volcano. Kim had to admit it was pretty realistic, with little trees dotted about on it.

Kim took out her bottle of oil and water, and checked that the blue coloring was in the bottom. Ella stared at it. "What is that?"

"You'll see," Kim said.

Mr. Smith walked slowly around the tables, watching the experiments. Two volcanoes didn't work very well. As he came closer, Kim got her flashlight ready and took out the special ingredient.

Next to her, Ella set off her volcano. Red foam erupted from the top, and so did half a dozen chocolate balls, springing out and bouncing down the sides like rocks.

"Wow!" said Mr. Smith. "That is amazing."

Kim frowned. Mr. Smith moved along to her. "What do we have here?"

Kim turned on the flashlight, took the lid off her bottle and tipped in the antacid tablets. In a few seconds, blue bubbles started rolling up and down the bottle. With Dad's big flashlight, it looked beautiful. Mr. Smith smiled. But was it a first-prize smile?

He moved on and finally got to Tom. Kim watched carefully. Tom was giggling again. He had a plain plastic bottle with nothing much in it. Just some little dots of things at the bottom.

"What's this?" Mr. Smith asked.

"Guess!" Tom said. He took the lid off and a disgusting smell filled the air.

Mr. Smith turned green and everyone
screwed up their noses.

"Ew! Yuck!" Tom had made a stink
bomb!

"I knew it!" Kim said. She started
toward Tom, but her elbow caught
the lava lamp and knocked it over.

A huge puddle of oil ran across the table and onto the floor.

Mr. Smith had a big hanky over his face. He looked like he was going to be sick! Everyone was running for the door, but they started slipping over in the cooking oil.

Kim grabbed Tom's bottle. "Hey!" Tom yelled, but it was too late. She raced outside and threw the bottle as far as she could.

By the time they could go back into the hall, everyone had given up on the science competition. Kim put the lid back on what was left of her lava lamp.

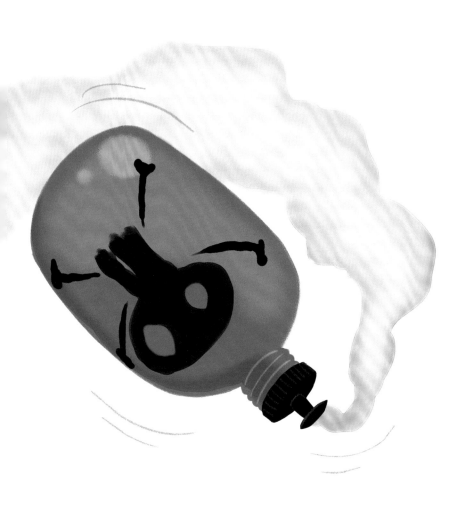

Mr. Smith was so upset that he had taken his camera and gone home. Nobody had won, and lots of people had oil all over them.

Kim walked home with Ella, helping her carry the volcano. What could she write for her blog this week?

Nothing had turned out right.
Except ... disasters were just what
a reporter reported best. She actually
had plenty to write about!

Kim's Email

From: kim_getthescoop@litols.com
To: haley86@litols.com
Sent: Sunday, March 7
Subject: My Super Science Project

Hi Haley,

How's your blog going? Last week I had a chance to win a video camera. All I had to do was produce the best science project. I tried lots of different things. Invisible ink. A glowing fountain in a drink bottle. A lava lamp. None of them won. Oh well. It gave me something to write about on my blog. Here's a picture of my lava lamp.

ttfn
Kim XOXO

MORE LEGENDS!

Want to find out about my next big scoop? Read my next book! Here's what happens...

Kim's town is full of weird pets: fat cats, crooked snakes, hairless dogs. When a prized pet goes missing, can "super reporter" Kim solve the mystery?

Meet the Author

Sherryl Clark loved to write letters when
she was a kid. She had penpals all over the
world (and wrote to her favorite author).
Now she loves blogging, writing, and reading,
and likes news about real people doing interesting
things. She also likes taking photos and writing
poems to go with them. She grew up in a tiny
country town and knows what it's like to live
where everybody knows everything about you!
Visit her at www.sherrylclark.com.

Meet the Illustrator

Heath McKenzie is a best-selling illustrator of picture books, novels, magazine art, and advertising and once even had his designs incorporated into jewelry. He most enjoys drawing zombies and dragons, but finds he just doesn't get nearly enough opportunities to do so! He lives in Melbourne, Australia, with his wife and baby daughter — and a small but loud dog. Oh, and he has a website you may enjoy. Visit him at: heathmck.com.

Read all the books in Set 2